ALEXANDER HAMILTON

YOUNG STATESMAN

Written by

Helen Boyd Higgins

Illustrated by Cathy Morrison

ISBN 978-1-882859-61-0 hardback
ISBN 978-1-882859-62-7 paperback

Patria Press, Inc.
PO Box 752
Carmel IN 46082
www.patriapress.com

Printed and bound in the United States of America
10 9 8 7 6 5 4 3 2 1

Text originally published by the Bobbs-Merrill Company, 1942, in the Childhood

of Famous Americans Series®. The Childhood of Famous Americans Series® is a

registered trademark of Simon & Schuster, Inc.

Library of Congress Cataloguing-in-Publication Data

Higgins, Helen Boyd.
    [Alec Hamilton, the Little Lion]
    Alexander Hamilton, young statesman / by Helen Boyd Higgins ; illustrated
by Cathy Morrison.
        p. cm. – (Young patriots series ; v. 14)
    Summary: Provides a fictional account of the childhood of the man who
would become the first Secretary of the Treasury, as he enjoys peaceful days
with his books and pet parrot on Caribbean islands, dreaming of one day
attending college in the American Colonies.
    ISBN-13: 978-1-882859-61-0 (hardcover)
    ISBN-13: 978-1-882859-62-7 (pbk.)
    1. Hamilton, Alexander, 1757-1804–Childhood and youth–Juvenile fiction.
[1. Hamilton, Alexander, 1757-1804–Childhood and youth–Fiction. 2. Family
life–Virgin Islands of the United States–Fiction. 3. Schools–Fiction. 4.
Conduct of life–Fiction. 5. Virgin Islands of the United States–History–
18th century–Fiction.] I. Morrison, Cathy, ill. II. Title.
    PZ7.H53495Al 2008
    [Fic]–dc22
                                    2007035676

Edited by Harold Underdown
Design by: Timothy Mayer/TM Design

This book is printed on Glatfelter's 55# Natural recycled paper.

Contents

Illustrations

To my father
Whose interest in the lives
Of great men became mine

Chapter 1

Rescue from the Sea

T he birds and monkeys heard Alec as he came running through the forest.

"Hey! My friends up there in the trees!" he shouted. "Do you know what day this is? It's my mother's birthday!"

The bright-colored, long-tailed parakeets twittered and the monkeys chattered, and Alexander Hamilton laughed as he jumped over a fallen log.

It was early morning on the island of St. Croix in the West Indies. St. Croix belonged to Denmark, unlike Nevis Island, where Alec was born, which belonged to England.

Alec watched as a long, greenish-brown snake uncoiled itself from the middle of the path and rattled away into the deep woods.

A land crab crawled across the path, and Alec sat down on the log to watch it. He began to sing, as he always did when he was excited. This morning he was thinking about his mother's birthday, so this is what he sang:

"It is the month of August
In seventeen sixty-five.
It is my mother's birthday —
I'm glad she is alive."

The crab kept pushing his heavy shell through the leaves.

"Goodbye," Alec called, "I'd like to follow you. But I don't have time today. I must find a piece of pink coral to tie on my mother's necklace. That will be my present for her."

As he spoke, a piece of coconut shell hit him on the ear. A family of monkeys was peeping down through the palm branches. They were throwing whatever their paws could reach.

Alec gave a shout and climbed up the nearest banana tree.

When he reached the branches just opposite the monkeys, he looked around for ammunition. Just above him was a giant bunch of ripe bananas.

"Hey!" he called to the little brown animals. "On guard, there! I'm fighting for the King."

The monkeys seemed to understand. Coconut pieces and bananas began to fly back and forth. It was a hard but short war.

"Come on, lazy ones!" Alec sh

the monkeys were hurrying away

"Hi-ho!" he called again as he

"I have won the battle for King

trees and this island of St. Cr

England."

ran down *oozed b* *wall*

The monkeys only chattered as they hurried away. Alec slid down the smooth tree trunk and ran happily up a steep path leading to a cliff overlooking the great, blue Atlantic Ocean.

Alec often came here just to watch the waves come tumbling in on the sandy beaches below. He liked to think about the time when he would take a boat across this ocean to the American Colonies.

His mother had told him that the American Colonies were so far away across the ocean that it took weeks to reach them. Alec knew that there were Indians living in the forests that covered much of the new land.

He also knew that in a town called New York in the new country, there was a college. Alec thought that it would be more exciting than anything in the whole world to sail away on a boat to America. It was his biggest dream.

But today he had no time to think about anything but his errand to the coral beach beyond the cliff. He

he path to the sandy shore. The wet sand
etween his toes. He turned a handspring and
ed into the sea.

He could hear the boom of the big ocean waves as they broke against the rocks at the entrance to the harbor. The water came higher and higher on his legs.

When it was up to his waist, Alec dove into the breakers. He swam with the waves into the deep, still water beyond.

Turning over on his back, he squinted at the soft clouds above him. Again he began to sing:

"The waves are soft and green and cold;
The sea is salt and oh! so old.
The fish that live beneath the water
Swim and swim and swim
And so do I."

He heard a gentle slapping of the water. It was very quiet. For a few minutes Alec forgot that he was on a special errand.

"Hurry-Up! Hurry-Up!" came the sound of a voice from close by.

Alec turned over on his side. He raised his head.

"Hurry-Up, Hurry-Up, Hurry-Up," the call came again.

"I'm coming," Alec shouted back. "Where are you?"

This time there was no answer. Alec swam around a point of land. He could see no one.

"Hi!" he called. "Where are you?"

Still he could see nothing but a few gulls flying close to the water looking for fish.

He shaded his eyes from the sun. Then he saw a small, dark object bobbing up and down on the waves, close to the coral rocks.

"Well!" Alec said. "I don't know what that can be. But I don't see anything else. The shout couldn't come from that, could it?"

"Hurry-Up. I say, matey," came the voice again.

"I'll go see what that is," Alec decided.

Alec was a fast swimmer. He was soon close beside the object. It was a cage-like box.

Alec pulled it toward him.

"Hi, matey!" came a voice from inside.

Alec was so surprised that he jerked back his arm.

There, peeping out at him, were two bright eyes. Looking at him from the corner of the box was a big green and red parrot.

"How did you get in there?" Alec asked as he pulled the box toward him.

The bird only blinked his eyes and ruffled his feathers.

Alec pushed the cage ahead of him toward the

shore. The bird scolded whenever the water came inside his house.

When Alec reached the shore he pushed the box high up on the sand. It was built to look like a small house. It had a slanted roof which was painted green. Alec saw some letters under the eaves of the roof.

HURRY-Up

HIS MAJESTY'S SAILING SHIP, *Altha.*

LONDON TO CHRISTIANSTED

1765

"Why, Hurry-Up must be your name! Do you want to get out?" he asked the bird.

The parrot snapped his bill and blinked his eyes. Alec pulled back the fastening which opened the door and Hurry-Up walked out on the sand. He waddled off down the shore, scolding and shaking his feathers.

Alec laughed and watched him go. Then, keeping one eye on the strange bird, he began to search among the piles of seaweed for a piece of pink coral.

After a while he decided to go around the point. Hurry-Up was sitting in the sun cleaning his feathers. Alec thought that the parrot was paying no attention to what he was doing. He started off down the shore.

"Hi, matey!" screamed the bird.

Alec turned. Hurry-Up was half flying and half

running down the sand toward him.

When the parrot reached Alec's side, he scolded and cawed. Alec stooped down to smooth his feathers, and the bird hopped up on his shoulder.

In a few minutes Hurry-Up flew down on the sand and began pushing and pulling the piles of seaweed about with his bill.

Alec laughed and laughed as he watched the busy bird.

"My! I hope that no one claims you! I want you for my pet. We could have a lot of fun together," he said.

The bird blinked and went on working.

It was getting late.

"I must find that coral. My present for Mother won't be pretty without it," Alec said with a frown.

"Hi, matey!" said the parrot. The bird had a piece of shell in his bill.

"No, that's not right. It has to be pink," Alec said as he took the shell and put it in his pocket.

Again the bird started hunting. Each time he found something, he brought it to Alec.

The sun was getting hot. Alec had a whole pocket full of things that Hurry-Up had found, but no pink coral.

"I won't give up," said Alec. "I won't."

"Hi, matey!" called Hurry-Up again from down the shore.

"We'll have to hurry if we want to get back to
Uncle Peter's before lunch is ready," Alec said. . .

"What did you find this time?" Alec said.
Hurry-Up came squawking toward him. He had

something pink in his bill.

"Hey!" shouted Alec. "You've found it! You've found the pink coral! That's wonderful! We don't have to hunt any more. Now we can go home."

But the parrot liked the game that he thought they had been playing. He didn't want to stop, and when Alec put him back in his box, he scolded and fussed. He scolded all the way across the narrow waterway to the home shore.

When they reached the shore, Alec let Hurry-Up out of his box. Alec could tell by the sun that it was almost noon.

"We'll have to hurry if we want to get back to Uncle Peter's before lunch is ready," Alec said as he started off through the woods with his new pet on his shoulder and the box in his hand.

Chapter 2

Happy Birthday, Mother

When Alec and Hurry-Up reached his Uncle Peter's plantation, the dinner bell was ringing.

This first signal meant that the field slaves, working in the sugar cane, were to stop, have lunch, and rest. It also meant that Alec's lunch would be ready in a half an hour.

He ran across the garden and up the stairs to his room. He dropped Hurry-Up on the bed and brought out a small iron box from the closet.

Inside the box was a string of tiny shells on a silk cord.

He lifted out the necklace and tied the pink coral to the middle of the string. Hurry-Up waddled over to the box and stuck his head inside.

"I found that box on the shore," Alec said, "near my own home before we moved here. This isn't my real home, you know, Hurry-Up."

The bird hopped up on Alec's knee. He picked at the necklace and tried to remove the coral.

"I know you found it," Alec said. "But we are giving it to Mother. Hey, don't do that!"

Hurry-Up began to shake the string of shells. He braced his feet and began to scold. Alec laughed. Hurry-Up scolded louder. His head went back and forth, and the shells tinkled like bells.

"Say, you have a temper just like mine, don't you, old fellow?" said Alec. "But you can't have the coral, even if you did find it."

Alec spoke so sternly that the bird blinked his eyes, let go of the coral, and flew off across the room.

Alec was still tying the coral when he heard his mother's voice outside. She was asking Becca, the maid, where he was.

Alec frowned. He knew that he must hurry because in his new home, he had to change his clothes before he went down to dinner. That was one reason Alec liked his old home best.

When he and his mother had lived on Nevis Island they had not dressed for dinner and they had eaten wherever they were. His little goat had come up on the terrace and Alec had squatted down by her side and had sent the warm milk right into his mouth.

Here his milk was served in a cup.

At Uncle Peter's big house he had to sit at a table.

He could not speak unless someone spoke to him. He could not leave the table until Uncle Peter and his mother were finished.

"*Squawk, squawk,*" came a funny sound from across the room. "*Gurgle, gurgle, gur—*"

Alec looked up from his work.

The water pitcher on the washstand was shaking back and forth. The parrot's two small, red feet waved feebly out of the mouth of the pitcher.

Alec hurried to pull him out. His eyes were closed and his head hung limp.

"Say, you better stop being so curious. You almost drowned," said Alec.

Hurry-Up shook his feathers. He choked and coughed. He started to scold and pecked at Alec's hand.

The big dinner bell rang again. Dinner was ready. Alec put Hurry-Up on the window sill and quickly pulled on his clean suit. Uncle Peter expected him to be on time for dinner.

He set Hurry-Up on his shoulder and ran down the iron steps from his balcony to the terrace below.

As he hurried he saw his mother reading in the garden.

"Mother, Mother!" he shouted. "Happy birthday, Mother! I have brought you a present. I made it myself. Last year on your birthday you said that you wanted one."

Alec threw his arms about his mother's neck and gave her a big hug. Then he put the necklace in her hand.

"Why, Alec, dear," she said. "It's beautiful! It must have taken you—"

"*Squawk, squawk,*" said Hurry-Up from Alec's shoulder.

The bird dove, picked up the necklace from the lady's hand, and flew off into a tall palm tree.

For a moment Alec and his mother were so surprised, they couldn't speak.

"Bring that back!" shouted Alec. "Bring it back!"

But the parrot only shook his wings and sat hunched up on the limb of the tree. The necklace hung from his bill.

"Where did that bird come from?" asked Alec's mother. "Oh, dear! My beautiful necklace!"

"Don't worry, I'll get it, Mother. Just you wait!" Alec shouted as he ran toward the tree.

His mother followed him and stood under the palm tree while Alec climbed up the smooth trunk.

As Alec got closer to Hurry-Up, the bird began to flutter his wings.

"Don't you fly to another tree!" shouted Alec. "I'll follow you if you do."

But instead of flying away, as Alec expected, Hurry-Up began to come toward Alec. When the two met, Alec held out his hand to catch the bird. Hurry-Up ducked his head and dropped the necklace quickly into the outstretched hand. Then he hopped upon his new friend's shoulder and began to squawk.

"Mother!" called Alec. "I think that Hurry-Up thought that you were taking the necklace away from me. He found part of it himself. Wait until I tell you how it happened."

When Alec reached the ground, he told his mother all about his morning's adventures. They were still laughing over the story when Uncle Peter called to them from the terrace. Then both of them felt a little guilty because they were late to dinner.

The table was set in the shade of a big palm tree which stood near the terrace. Poleon, a young slave just Alec's age, stood behind Alec's mother's chair waving a palm branch over the table. He had to do this at all the meals to keep the flies away.

Alec pushed in his mother's chair and went quickly around the table to his own. Hurry-Up was settled on his shoulder.

Everything went smoothly until Hurry-Up flapped his wings and dove into a dish for a piece of food.

Poleon tried to catch him but the bird flew onto Uncle Peter's shoulder.

Alec ran around the table to catch his pet. He expected Uncle Peter to be very angry.

Poleon, a young slave just Alec's age, stood behind Alec's mother's chair waving a palm branch over the table.

"Well! Well!" was all the older man said.

Then Alec saw that Uncle Peter was laughing so hard that he could hardly get his breath. Alec and his mother looked at each other. Then they began to laugh, too. Hurry-Up began to caw.

Uncle Peter lifted the bird from his shoulder and began to stroke his feathers.

"Where did you get him?" he asked Alec. "I once had a parrot. An old sailor gave it to me. I taught him to sing and say all kinds of things."

"I found him floating in a little box out beyond the coral rocks this morning," said Alec. "On the box it said that his name was Hurry-Up."

"Hurry-Up," said the bird. "Hi, matey!"

Uncle Peter smiled. Then they went back to eating. For the first time, Uncle Peter let Alec talk at the table.

It was the nicest meal that Alec and his mother had had since they had left home.

For dinner, besides turtle, they had yams, guava jelly, goat's milk, and pineapple.

When they had finished, Uncle Peter sat with them for a few minutes.

"The *Queen Bess* will dock tomorrow, Rachel," he said to Alec's mother. "You'll soon have your silk and linen from England."

"Oh, Uncle Peter, may Poleon and I go with you to

the landing? Please let us," said Alec.

"Why, you have been to many a landing, I'm sure, haven't you, Alec?" asked Uncle Peter.

"Oh, yes, sir," said Alec. "But my book is on the *Queen Bess*. Please, please, let us go with you."

"Books. Books. Don't you ever think of anything but books, nephew? You read too much—and I don't like begging."

"I didn't mean to beg, only—"

"Then don't," said Uncle Peter.

"But Uncle Peter—"

"Alec!" said his mother.

Uncle Peter went into the house.

"Oh, Mother, please! I just must go. I— "

"Alexander!"

Alec stopped. When his mother spoke to him that way there was no use begging.

"You and Poleon go and get your rest," said his mother.

Even though Alec and Poleon were eight years old, they still took a nap after dinner. Everyone did. Even the men and women who worked in the fields and the men who worked in the warehouse by the docks took naps.

The two boys ran to where a hammock hung beneath a tree.

Alec climbed inside. Poleon lay down on the ground.

For a few minutes they were both quiet. Then Alec began to speak.

"Poleon," he began, "do you want to go away with me to the American Colonies?"

"Do I want to do what?" asked Poleon.

"Do you want to get on a boat with me some day, and go away across the Atlantic Ocean and—"

Poleon didn't answer. He was asleep. Alec settled back into the hammock to dream about the time when he would cross the ocean.

"Tomorrow," he said to himself, "I'll have a book that will tell me all about that new country. I hope Uncle Peter will let me go to the landing. I wonder. . . ."

Then Alec went to sleep.

Chapter 3

The Boat Lands, and Alec Makes a Friend

The next morning Poleon woke Alec before it was quite light.

"Master Alec! Master Alec!" he whispered. "We're going to see the *Queen Bess* come in. Better get up!"

Alec jumped out of bed before his eyes were wide open. Poleon was dressed in his best shirt and pants. He was grinning.

"So Uncle Peter changed his mind?" Alec asked as he ran to the closet for his good suit and shoes.

"You going to put on your shoes, too, Master Alec? You're bound to slip on them dock boards if you do," Poleon said.

"Poleon, you know Uncle Peter won't let me go into town without my shoes and white shirt. That's the only thing I hate about a ship landing."

Alec scrubbed his face and put on a shirt with ruffles down the front.

When they reached the terrace, Poleon ran off to eat with his grandfather, old Poleon, who was Uncle Peter's coachman.

"Now," said Uncle Peter as Alec slipped into his chair, "you look like a gentleman."

"My feet hurt," said Alec.

Uncle Peter paid no attention to what Alec said. Alec's mother was not at the table. The two ate in silence.

After breakfast Becca gave each of them a heavy shawl to wrap about their shoulders to keep them warm. Old Poleon tucked the shawls about them and the horses started off on the six-mile trip to Christiansted. The *Queen Bess* would come into the harbor of this busy town. Little Poleon snuggled down next to his grandfather on the high carriage seat.

Alec watched everything that they passed. He leaned out of the window to watch the mist come in from the ocean. He watched the dark green of the palm branches turn to a lighter color when the sun touched them.

When the road wound near High Cliffs, Uncle Peter said that the horses must rest.

"May we go and see if the *Queen Bess* is coming into the harbor, Uncle Peter?" Alec said.

Uncle Peter nodded. Alec and Poleon ran to the edge of the cliff. The *Queen Bess* was in sight. A strong wind filled her sails.

"Uncle Peter! Uncle Peter!" Alec shouted as the two raced back to the carriage. "She is coming into the harbor. Hurry!"

Uncle Peter shook his head.

"The horses must rest," he said.

So Alec and Poleon had to wait until the horses stopped their hard breathing. Then they started down the road.

"Uncle Peter," said Alec after they had been driving for a long time, "what do we have in the hold of the ship today?"

"Tools for the plantation and linen and silk for your mother," Uncle Peter answered. "Then there is a new harness for my horse Prince."

"And my book," finished Alec. He said it very softly, but Uncle Peter frowned and stopped talking.

When they reached the edge of the town they went slowly because there were no sidewalks and many people were in town to meet the ship.

Alec and Poleon hung out the sides of the carriage so that they would miss nothing that there was to see.

They saw a man with a trained monkey and another selling fresh figs and big grass hats. A tall, thin sailor had a small whistle in his mouth. He played tunes and children gathered about him. More than once the carriage had to stop.

. . .there were no sidewalks and many people were
in town to meet the ship.

"Uncle Peter, could we get out and walk? We would get there quicker," said Alec.

Uncle Peter nodded and told old Poleon where to meet them after the boat landed. Then young Poleon, Alec, and Uncle Peter got out of the carriage and pushed their way through the crowd.

A group of sailors shoved them aside. These men were speaking a strange language.

"I wish I could understand what they are saying," Alec said. "I don't like it when people say things that I can't understand."

Uncle Peter smiled at his nephew.

"You could learn to speak that language if you tried. It is called Portuguese. But you don't need to. All those men can speak English as well as their own language."

"I don't like them to be able to do what I can't do," said Alec.

"Make way! Make way!" shouted many voices behind them.

A line of two-wheeled wagons, pulled by slave boys, came by.

"Those are Cruger's wagons," said Uncle Peter. "They meet every boat. They carry all the goods which Mr. Cruger has ordered for his big warehouse. And there is Nicholas Cruger himself."

Alec looked. He saw a short, heavy-set man

dressed in white. He had on a big grass hat and was smoking a long, black cigar. He nodded to Uncle Peter and hurried on.

The ship's bells were ringing. The *Queen Bess* was landing.

Alec stayed close to Uncle Peter. He wanted to see all that would happen when the *Queen Bess* landed.

He watched the sailors throw the big ropes over the side of the boat to men on the dock. Another bell rang. One white sail after the other came racing down the pole.

Exotic-looking people, all men, stood along the rail of the ship. They were traders who came and went from the American Colonies to the West Indies and to England.

They were all anxious to come ashore. Some of them called to people whom they knew on the dock.

Alec saw a tall, dark-skinned man standing by the opening where the gangplank would soon be pushed. He had on gold earrings, and there was a scar across his face.

Mr. Cruger's little wagons were all lined up before the boat. All other wagons had to wait until these were filled.

A thin young man with a pencil in his hand and his pockets full of papers pushed against Uncle Peter.

"Excuse me, sir," he said. "I must be ready to check

the goods that Mr. Cruger has ordered. We have a great deal on the *Queen Bess* today."

Uncle Peter nodded.

"Mr. Andrews, this is my nephew, Alexander Hamilton," he said.

Alec held out his hand but Mr. Andrews was already too busy checking the first load of goods to see it.

A small wooden keg was near Mr. Andrews. Alec climbed on top of this so that he could look over Mr. Andrews's shoulder. He wanted to see what Mr. Cruger's clerk would put down on the paper.

From this position, Alec could also see far over the crowd. He saw a tall man, with no hat on his large head, coming through the pushing, jamming gang of men. He saw this stranger clap men on the shoulders. He could see that each person to whom he spoke smiled and moved aside.

As the stranger came closer, he looked up and saw Alec. They both smiled and Alec wished that he knew this man. Just as he wished this, he heard Uncle Peter say, "Good morning to you, Preacher Knox."

"Good morning, Mr. Peter Lytton. A good day to you, sir."

"I suppose you are expecting more books on board the *Queen Bess*. Am I right?" Uncle Peter said with a smile.

"You are, sir. A finer order I have never sent to London. I sold my gold watch to pay for them."

"Your gold watch, sir!" said Alec. "Your watch! Oh!"

Hugh Knox smiled at Alec.

"Does that surprise you, young man?" he said.

"Oh yes, sir. A gold watch is. . . well. . . ."

"This is my nephew, Mr. Knox," said Uncle Peter. "The lad has one of your great failings, sir. I think he would trade his uncle for a book. Wouldn't you, Alec?"

"I might if the book were about the American Colonies," Alec answered.

Both men laughed and Alec knew that his uncle was not angry with him for what he had said.

"Well, well," said Mr. Knox. "What do you know about the American Colonies, young man?"

"I know very little. But my mother ordered a book which tells all about them. It is on the *Queen Bess*. I came down to get it."

"Mr. Knox, Mr. Knox," called a loud voice from nearer the boat. "Here is a parcel for you."

"I'll be right with you, my man," shouted Mr. Knox.

Then he turned to Alec.

"Shall I get your package, too?" he asked.

Alec nodded, too excited to speak. Mr. Knox hurried off through the crowd.

"I must see about my packages," said Uncle Peter. "I want you to stay right here, Alec. Right here on this box. Is that understood?"

"Yes, sir," Alec answered, still looking at Mr. Knox's broad shoulders.

He saw a porter give his new friend a box. Then he saw that Mr. Knox was asking questions. He saw the sailor nod and start looking through a pile of parcels in a cart. Alec saw Mr. Knox take a small paper bundle, slip it into his pocket, and turn toward where Alec waited.

"Here it is, Alexander," Mr. Knox shouted.

He started through the crowd to come back to Alec, but several men stopped him. Alec saw him listen to what they had to say. Then he saw Mr. Knox turn, and without once looking his way, start off with the strangers.

"Mr. Knox! Mr. Knox!" shouted Alec.

Alec's voice was drowned in all the noise. The minister was leaving, with Alec's package in his pocket.

Alec jumped down from the box and started to push his way through the crowd. He slipped. The soles of his shoes were slippery.

Poleon had been right. It was awful to have to wear shoes.

Alec dared not stop. He was afraid that if he did,

he would lose sight of Mr. Knox.

"I've got to catch up with him," Alec said to himself.

Even then he did not remember that Uncle Peter had told him to stay where he was.

Chapter 4

The Chase

"**M**r. Knox! Mr. Knox!" Alec shouted.

The tall man didn't stop. Alec began to cough because of all the dust in the air. He slipped again.

He came to the place where the main street crossed another road. Mr. Knox was on the other side, but Alec could not cross because the crowd was held up by a slow-moving ox cart.

"Mr. Knox! Mr. Knox!" he called.

"Lose somebody, young feller?" a sailor asked.

Alec didn't answer because the crowd was moving again. He was shoved and pushed. He stumbled across the street. He could not see Mr. Knox. He began to shout. But he was so far down in the crowd that no one could see or hear him.

Alexander Hamilton shut his teeth hard. He blinked back the tears. His mouth was bleeding where someone had struck him.

Then, suddenly, there was a clear space, and, not

far ahead, was Mr. Knox. He had stopped to talk. Alec jumped ahead, slipped, and fell. For a moment he thought that he would be stepped on by the heavy feet around him. He rolled to the other side of the road.

He started to get up. Then, as the way seemed clearer down near the ground, he began to crawl.

"Mr. Knox! Mr. Knox!" he shouted.

This time his voice carried.

Mr. Knox turned and came striding back. He stopped and pulled Alec to the side of the road.

"What are you doing here?" he asked.

"My book!" Alec answered. "My book, Mr. Knox. I was afraid you were going to forget it was mine."

"Mr. Knox," called one of the sailors, "they are wanting you back at the store. Are you coming?"

"Aye," shouted Mr. Knox. "Come on, Alexander, you better come along with me."

The big man pushed forward. Alec's eyes danced. He had to run to keep up with his new friend.

They hurried through the door of the warehouse. A crowd of men stood back as they came into the room.

"Here comes Preacher Knox. Let him by," shouted a loud voice. "Come this way, sir. It's an argument we want you to settle."

The minister stepped into the center of the circle of men. Two of them stood face to face, frowning. Alec recognized the larger of the two as the man with earrings whom he had seen on the *Queen Bess.*

The other was much smaller. He wore lace ruffles and he had his hair tied back with a black ribbon.

It was hard for Alec to see because he was so short. Everyone was pushing and trying to get near the two in the center of the crowd.

Alec quickly found a table on which he could stand. When he had climbed up he could see right over the heads of the others.

"Now," he heard Mr. Knox say, "what is all the trouble?"

The big man shook his fist at the smaller man.

"He say they no more Spain in that American Colonies," he shouted. "And I say they no more France in that country of American Colonies."

"And I, Monsieur DuVanne, know that you are wrong. The great treaty of peace was signed in my Paris."

"But France lost all its land in North America. It lost Senegal in Africa and its power in India, too," came a small shrill voice.

Everyone turned toward the table where Alec stood. He went on.

"All the French land was divided between the British and the Spanish," he continued. "That was two years ago, in 1763."

The men were so surprised that they stood with their

mouths open. The smaller man looked frightened.

"Alexander," said Mr. Knox. "How do you know that is so?"

"I know it because my mother told me all about the Treaty of Paris," Alec answered.

As the crowd pushed about him, Alec kept on speaking. Alec loved to have people listen to him.

Mr. Knox stood quietly by his side. The minister was surprised at Alec's answers.

"This is a wonderful boy," he said to himself. "I must teach him."

The crowd increased. Men pushed close to listen. Alec pushed back his hair with his small brown hand and answered questions.

Suddenly the crowd drew back.

"Alexander!" said a new voice.

It was Uncle Peter. He looked very angry.

"Come with me," he said.

Then, for the first time, Alec remembered that his uncle had told him to stay on the box near the boat. He stopped talking and got down from the table. The crowd began to disappear.

"I'm sorry, Uncle Peter," said Alec as he hurried after his Uncle. "I didn't mean to disobey you. I—"

Uncle Peter paid no attention. Alec looked at Mr. Knox and they both followed the older man from the room.

"What will he do to me?" thought Alec. "Oh, I hope that he won't take away my book. I hope—"

By this time they had all reached the warehouse door.

Poleon and the carriage were waiting outside the warehouse.

"I'll go along with you, Peter Lytton, if you'll have me for supper," said Mr. Knox.

Uncle Peter only nodded. The three climbed into the carriage, making the seat very crowded. Alec sat in the middle. The horses started.

Uncle Peter closed his eyes. Mr. Knox looked the other way. Alec felt miserable and didn't know what to do or say. He wondered what Uncle Peter would do to him when they reached home. Would he take away his book? Would he be punished?

He leaned closer to Mr. Knox. As he did so he felt something hard against his side. It must be his book. Alec sat up straight. Uncle Peter seemed to be asleep.

"Mr. Knox," he whispered. "May I have my book?"

Mr. Knox jumped. Then he smiled at Alec and put his hand down into his pocket.

"I'll take that package," said Uncle Peter.

"But Uncle Peter. It is mine. I—"

"I'll take that package, Mr. Knox," Uncle Peter said sternly. "I'll take it. No boy who deliberately disobeys deserves a present."

"But I didn't mean—"

Mr. Knox handed the parcel to Uncle Peter. Alec's eyes flashed. He clenched his hands.

"That isn't fair! It is my book. I worked for it. Give it to me!" he said.

"Alexander!"

Alec swallowed hard.

"You can punish me if you want to," Alec answered, "but it isn't fair to take my book."

Uncle Peter put the small package behind the seat. Then he closed his eyes. Alec started to argue, but Mr. Knox shook his head.

Alec stuck his hands into his pockets and kept silent. It seemed a long time until the carriage came to the home plantation.

It stopped at the door. Mr. Knox was the first out. Then Alec jumped over the bundles and started to run.

"Alexander!" called Uncle Peter.

Alec stopped. He turned around slowly and came back.

"Alexander, you will go to your room and remain there until morning. You will have no supper," Uncle Peter said.

"I want my book. You have no right—"

"Go to your room!" said Uncle Peter.

Alec burst into angry tears. He stamped up the steps and banged open the door to his room.

"He hasn't any right! He hasn't any right!" he shouted as he threw himself across the bed and began to pound the pillow.

"Hi, matey!" said a voice near by.

"Get out of here!" Alec shouted to Hurry-Up.

The bird flew to the washstand and began to squawk and flap his wings.

Alec kicked his feet and went on pounding the pillow.

It was the first time that he had lost his temper in many months.

"Hurry-Up," said the parrot from across the room.

Alec jumped to his feet and began pacing up and down. He walked to the window and heard his mother talking to Uncle Peter.

"But, Peter," he heard her say, "what happened? I haven't heard the little lion roar for a long time. I don't know when I have seen him so angry."

Alec walked away from that side of the room.

"If I'm a little lion," he said, "I wish that I could do more than roar."

Back and forth and back and forth, Alec tramped.

"Hurry-Up, Hurry-Up, Hurry-Up," said a voice behind him. Alec turned around. There was the parrot strutting along after him. He was breathless from

It was the first time that he had lost his temper
in many months.

trying to keep up with his friend.

When Alec stopped, the bird stopped. He looked up
at his friend and blinked his eyes. He put his head on
one side and scolded.

At this Alec began to laugh. He picked up his pet
and began to smooth his feathers. Then he lay down

on the bed and was soon asleep. The parrot pushed close to his shoulder and went to sleep, too.

When Alec's mother came up, she was surprised and pleased to see a smile on the boy's face. As she leaned over Alec's bed, she said softly, "If only Mr. Knox could help my boy to conquer his temper."

Alec was dreaming that Hurry-Up was waddling along behind him again. This time Hurry-Up was carrying the new book!

Chapter 5

I'll Not Be Afraid

When Alec woke the next morning, the sun was shining full in his face.

"Alexander!" came a deep voice from the terrace below.

It was his Uncle Peter calling. He was late for breakfast.

"Alexander Hamilton!" came the call again.

Alec sprang into his clothes, ran his hand through his hair, and rushed out the door. His uncle stood by the breakfast table.

"Good morning, Alexander," he said as Alec came to his side.

"Good morning, Uncle Peter. I—I didn't hear you at first. I—"

Alec gulped and cleared his throat. Until now he had forgotten yesterday's angry scene with his uncle. He gulped again and held out his hand.

"Uncle Peter, I'm sorry that I disobeyed you yesterday. I'm sorry that I lost my temper but—"

Alec stopped. He and Uncle Peter looked at each other and they both began to smile.

"Well," Uncle Peter began. "Maybe I was a mite hasty myself about that package, nephew."

When Alec's mother and Mr. Knox came out they found the two shaking hands.

After breakfast Uncle Peter spoke to Alec.

"I'd like to see you in my office, Alexander. I am going there now."

Alec looked at his mother. He wondered if she knew what Uncle Peter wanted. Was he still going to be punished?

But Alec's mother was talking to Mr. Knox and didn't look his way. So he followed his uncle toward the office on the other side of the garden.

The office was a small room with a long table in the center. About its walls on a shelf stood many model ships, which had been made for his uncle by sailors. A small new one of the *Queen Bess* had just been added to the collection.

Uncle Peter motioned to Alec to sit down across the table from him. Then he took a package from a drawer.

"Your mother tells me that you earned this book by learning certain lessons in French," he began.

"Yes, sir, I did. That was the reason that—" Alec

started to speak.

"I know, that was the reason that you thought you should have it. I'm beginning to think that you are quite right, nephew," he said with a smile as he handed the package to Alec.

Alec's hand shook as he began to untie the heavy knot.

In the package was a small book bound in soft leather. Alec settled back in his chair. He forgot that his uncle was in the room. He began to read.

"Ahem!" said Uncle Peter. "Before you finish the book, nephew, I want to talk to you," he said.

Alec looked up and met his uncle's twinkling eyes. He grinned and sat back in the chair with his fingers still in the place between the first pages.

"Alexander," began Uncle Peter, "I want you to begin to ride the cane for me."

Now Alec knew that to ride the cane meant to ride a horse day after day through the sugarcane fields to watch over the slaves working there. His face became white. He was afraid of horses.

"But Uncle Peter, I—" he started again.

"I know, Alec, you think that you are afraid of horses. I want to help you get over that feeling. You can never be quite the man that you want to be while you are afraid of anything. Riding the cane will help."

"I know, Alec, you think that you are afraid of horses.
I want to help you get over that feeling.

Alec stared at his uncle. His mouth became dry.
Uncle Peter went on.

"You say that you want to go to the American
Colonies to college. You could never do that with the
little education you have now. I want you to work for
your education and I want you to conquer your fear.
Riding the cane will do both."

Alec did not answer.

"When you have learned to ride a horse," his uncle went on, "I will let you go to Mr. Knox's school in Christiansted and. . . ."

"To school? To a real school? To learn everything that there is to learn so that I can go to college? Oh, Uncle Peter!" shouted Alec as he threw his arms around his uncle's neck.

"There! There!" said his uncle. "Give me a breath. You may ride the cane for me in the mornings. I will pay you for that. Then in the afternoons you may go to school. Will you do that?"

"Will I do it? Will I?" Alec pounded on the table because he was so excited. "Uncle Peter, I'll ride all day and study at night if you want."

Uncle Peter smiled. He put his arm about his nephew's shoulders.

"I believe you would, Alec," he said.

"And, Uncle Peter, I'll not let myself be afraid."

"And do you think that you can keep that temper of yours, my boy? That is your worst fault, you know," Uncle Peter asked.

"I will do my very best, Uncle Peter. My very best. You can count on me, sir."

"We'll see. We'll see," said Uncle Peter. "Come now, we'll go and tell your mother and Mr. Knox about our new plans."

Alec pushed open the office door. The two started

across the garden. When they came in sight of the house, Poleon began to shout from the drive.

"Look, Master Alec!" he called. "Just you look. It's yours!"

Chapter 6

Christopher Columbus

Alec stopped. There was Poleon holding the bridle of a small, black horse whose white feet were pawing the thick dust of the drive.

"For me?" Alec asked.

"For you, nephew," said Uncle Peter. "I thought it would be easier for you to ride the cane if you had a horse of your own. He is a good little horse and I know that you can learn to ride him."

"I will. I'll do anything if only I can go to school. Just anything that you say, sir."

Uncle Peter put his arm about his nephew's shoulders. Alec was shivering. He could never forget the time he had been thrown from a large horse and had been almost stepped on by the heavy feet above him.

Now, as he walked, Alec's knees trembled. He took a deep breath and almost ran to the horse, which backed and jerked at his halter.

"Not so fast, nephew," said Uncle Peter. "Never

There was Poleon holding the bridle of a small, black horse whose white feet were pawing the thick dust of the drive.

rush into a friendship, even with an animal. The horse doesn't know you, so he doesn't trust you."

"I didn't think. I was just going to pat him," Alec answered.

"Give him some of these cane pieces," Poleon said.

Alec took the pieces Poleon gave him and held them out to the restless animal, who came forward so quickly that Alec backed up, stumbled, and fell. The horse came on. Alec screamed and rolled to the side.

45

"Don't be scared," Poleon said. "He just wants to eat that cane."

Alec jumped to his feet. His eyes flashed and he went slowly to the horse with the pieces of sugar cane in his hand.

"What is his name, Uncle Peter?"

"Trotter. But if you don't like that name, you could give him another."

"Oh, I know just the name for him. I'll call him Christopher Columbus. Christy for short."

Uncle Peter smiled and looked surprised.

"Don't you see, Uncle Peter? If I call him that, then he and I would both like to discover places and things. And I could never be afraid again if I had Christopher Columbus as a friend," said Alec.

"Afraid? Who is afraid?" said a new voice.

Alec's mother and Mr. Knox were coming toward them.

"I *was* afraid of a horse, Mr. Knox," said Alec. "But I'm not going to be any longer."

Then Alec ran to his mother's side.

"Mother, Mother!" he shouted. "I'm going to ride the cane for Uncle Peter. Then, just as soon as I can do that and take care of my horse, I'm going to school. Mother, do you hear me? I'm going to a real school. To Mr. Knox's school in Christiansted."

Alec's mother smiled and gave her boy a hug.

"To my school?" said Mr. Knox. "To my school with Tom and Neddy Stevens and Benjamin Yard? Why, that's fine!"

"Are the boys about my age?" asked Alec. "I hope so."

"Just about, I should think," answered Mr. Knox. "Ben Yard may be a little older."

Alec nodded and began to pat Christy's neck. "Poleon, what should I do first, to learn to ride?" he asked.

"You better get yourself up into the saddle, Master Alec," said Poleon. "That's the only way I know to ride a horse."

Everyone laughed. Alec stepped up on the mounting block and pulled himself into the saddle. Old Poleon mounted Uncle Peter's horse, Prince. The old man put a lead strap on Christy and he and Alec went for the first lesson.

Alec rode all morning. He rested a little after dinner and was ready to start again.

When he came in at supper time, he was limping. His mother looked worried when she saw how hard it was for him to climb the steps.

"You have ridden too much today, Alec," she said.

"But, Mother, I have to hurry. Those boys at school will be ahead of me. Won't they, Mr. Knox?"

"I don't know how far along in your work you are,

young man," answered Mr. Knox.

"I'll show you how much I can read right now," Alec said.

"Not now, dear," said his mother. "Go get ready for supper."

Alec frowned but he started at once across the terrace. His legs hurt. His back hurt. His head ached.

"I'll be right down," he called back.

But when his mother sent Becca, the cook, up to see why he didn't come, she said that Alec was asleep on his bed.

It was late that night when Alec's mother woke him and helped him undress. She rubbed his back with some liniment.

"What time is it? Is Mr. Knox ready to hear me read?" Alec asked sleepily.

"It is very late, dear," answered Alec's mother. "You can read to Mr. Knox tomorrow."

◆

The next morning, Poleon came many times to try to waken Alec. It was nearly noon when he finally woke up on his own. His body hurt. His arms and legs ached. But he called for Poleon and sent him to tell his grandfather that Alec would ride today.

It was very hard for Alec to dress. It hurt to bend over. It hurt to straighten up. It hurt to sit down and it hurt to walk. He limped across the floor and out onto the balcony. There, he sat down at the top of the steps.

"I'm going to ride. I will ride," he said to himself.

He slid from step to step until he reached the terrace. It seemed a long way to where old Poleon was waiting with Christy. Alec found that he was so stiff that he could hardly mount alone.

"Now, Master Alec," said old Poleon, "you just better not—"

"Take the lead strap off today," Alec demanded. "I want to ride alone."

But the old man had had his orders from Uncle Peter. Alec was not to ride alone until he was much steadier than he was now.

Alec sat as straight as he could. He remembered as many of the directions he had been given as possible. But his head ached and the jog of Christy's gait sent pains through his body.

They rode until the plantation dinner bell rang.

"I'll go back now, Poleon," said Alec.

That afternoon Alec's mother, Mr. Knox, and Uncle Peter sat on the terrace. A little away from the others Alec sat, still sore, but reading. He heard nothing of what the older people were saying until Mr. Knox passed his chair waving his arms above his head.

"The American Colonies will be the greatest country on this earth, sir!" he shouted. "The power of the King will one day be taken over by the people themselves in that new country. You'll see."

"That might be treason, Knox," said Uncle Peter, rising quickly from his chair.

Alec slipped from his chair to stand near his mother.

"Treason, sir?" said Mr. Knox. "No, sir. No Englishman will pay a tax that he himself has not made. The King is imposing taxes on everything. The Stamp Act was passed only last month."

"Will there be war in America?" Alec asked.

"Maybe. Maybe. Here is a letter from my friend Hercules Mulligan. He lives in Boston Town. He is much worried over the troubles in the American Colonies. Read the letter out loud, young man," answered Mr. Knox.

Alec took the letter in his hand. He frowned.

"Go on," the young preacher urged.

"I can't read writing, sir," said Alec. "I can't even make my letters. When mother wanted to teach me, I didn't want to learn. I just wanted to read out of books."

"That's too bad. Maybe you aren't ready to come to my school. The boys know their letters and can read and write Latin and English."

"But I will learn. You'll see," said Alec.

He hurried off into the house and soon came back with everything he needed to take his first lesson.

"Please show me how to write my name and the word America, too," said Alec.

"*A* should be your favorite letter," Mr. Knox said with a chuckle. "*A* for America and for Alexander."

"*A* for America and for Alexander—that's wonderful! How do you write it?" asked Alec.

"You write it this way," answered Mr. Knox.

Then the minister made a copy for each letter.

"Now you try," said Mr. Knox.

Alec worked all afternoon. By supper time he knew his whole alphabet, but he still liked the *A's* best.

"I will soon be ready for your school," he said to Mr. Knox.

Mr. Knox smiled. He believed that Alec was right.

Chapter 7

Alec Has a Job

In a week's time, Alec rode without the lead strap. Old Poleon still jogged along by his side to tell him about the work in the cane fields.

He told him how the cane was planted and tended and cut. He showed him how the cane stalks were crushed between great stones that ground them into pulp. The juice ran out into an iron pipe which carried it to big kettles.

These kettles were placed over the fire, and when the juice was thick enough, it was put out in great flats in the sun. Here it changed into tiny, sparkling bits called sugar crystals.

Alec talked to the men and the women in the fields and asked questions of the foremen.

One morning, late in August, Alec and old Poleon were trotting along a path which was so narrow that they had to ride single file. Christy went ahead.

A troop of monkeys was playing among the trees

A troop of monkeys was playing among the
trees near the path.

near the path. As the horses passed, the monkeys threw bits of bark and small branches at them. One piece hit Christy's nose.

Christy reared and plunged. He dragged the loose reins from Alec's hands and bolted across the cane stubble.

Alec had forgotten to keep the steady hold old Poleon had taught him. His mind had been far away thinking.

His left foot began to slip from the stirrup. He leaned far to the side and grabbed Christy about the neck.

Old Poleon's big horse pounding along behind frightened Christy even more.

Suddenly, Alec realized that no one could help him but himself. For a minute he was terrified. Then he pulled himself together.

"Who-o-o-a!" he said quietly. "Who-o-a, Christy, don't be scared."

He pulled himself up a little at a time, pushed his foot back into the stirrup, and began to pull the reins to the right and then to the left.

Christy began to slow. Alec patted his neck. Christy came to a halt.

When old Poleon came up, both Christy and Alec were still trembling. Alec was pale, but his eyes sparkled. He smiled at the old man.

"Master Alec!" the old coachman cried. "Are you hurt!"

Alec grinned.

"Of course I'm not hurt. Christy and I were both pretty scared, that's all," he answered.

"I better put the lead strap back on him," said old Poleon .

"No, I'll never need that strap again. I know that I can ride now. Christy and I understand each other," said Alec.

That same day Alec went to see his Uncle Peter in his office.

"Uncle Peter," he said, "I can ride now. I can take care of a horse and I'm ready to help on the plantation."

Uncle Peter smiled and came around the desk to shake hands with his nephew.

"I think you can ride, nephew," the older man said, "but will the field hands do as you ask them to do?"

"They will, sir, I'm sure they will. I like them, Uncle Peter, and I think they like me. I know that I'll make a lot of mistakes, but I will try and keep my temper. If I lose it, I'll come and tell you at once. Then you can get someone else to take my place. Is that fair?"

"That's a bargain, nephew," Uncle Peter said. "You may start on the cane tomorrow and—"

"When may I go to school?" Alec broke in.

"Tomorrow afternoon."

Alec grabbed his uncle's hand, shook it hard, and rushed from the room.

"Mother, Mother!" he shouted as he ran across the garden. "Mother, I'm going to school tomorrow! Uncle Peter says that I may begin riding the cane tomorrow morning and then I may start school in the afternoon. Aren't you excited, Mother!"

"It's splendid, Alec dear. We ought to celebrate. What shall we do?"

"A picnic!" shouted Alec. "A picnic on the shore— oh, that would be fine. I'll go tell Becca to fix up a lunch, shall I?"

His mother nodded.

Alec began to sing as he ran up the stairs to change his clothes:

"A picnic, a picnic—
Supper by the sea.
A picnic, a picnic
For Mother and for me."

Chapter 8

School At Last

The picnic was a great success. Alec and his mother laughed and swam and ate Becca's good supper. When they reached home, they both felt happy. Alec's mother was tired, but he was still excited thinking about tomorrow.

The next morning, when Alec started off across the plantation, it was still dark. But the sun soon came up from the mists, and Alec rode along with the field workers, singing their chants.

At noon he came home, dressed, ate his dinner and hurried to say goodbye to his mother. She was still lying down, worn out from the picnic.

"Oh, Mother! I'm ready to go. Isn't it wonderful?" Alec said as he gave her a big hug.

"I think that I'm as excited as you are, dear," she answered. "I have wanted this for you for a long time. It will be hard work, son. The other boys are ahead of you."

"They won't be ahead for long," said Alec. "I'll work harder than any of them. You'll see."

"Hi, matey," said Hurry-Up as he settled down on Alec's shoulder.

"Shall I take him with me?" Alec asked as he smoothed his pet's feathers.

"I don't think that parrots and school would mix, do you?" laughed his mother.

Alec put the bird down on his mother's bed.

"Be fair with the boys, Alec. They have been together a long time. They may tease you," his mother warned. "Watch your—"

"Temper. I will. I promise you that."

"No, don't promise me; just do the best you can."

"I will. I really will, Mother," Alec called as he ran down the steps and out to the drive.

Christy was ready and they were soon galloping down the road.

When they came to the main highway, Alec pulled the little horse down to a walk.

"Suppose those other boys do know a great deal more than I do. Suppose they can beat me in everything. Then what?" he asked the horse.

Christy only flicked his ears.

Before they came to the drive that led to the minister's house, they came to a small bridge across a narrow stream. Christy was thirsty. Alec loosened the reins and waited impatiently as the little horse took a long drink.

"Get down off that horse!"

"Who do you think you are, riding to school on horseback?"

"Get off, I say!"

The shouts came from the bushes near by. Alec pulled Christy's head up and started back to the road. Three boys came dashing at him. They were shouting and screaming and brandishing long sticks.

Christy snorted and reared. Alec lost his balance and fell off at the feet of the three shouting boys, who began to laugh.

Alec sprang to his feet and Christy galloped off down the road.

"Stop that laughing!" Alec said sharply. "Stop it!"

The boys only laughed harder.

"Come on and make us," said a fat boy as he gave Alec a push down the hill.

The other boys laughed and began to jeer.

Alec sprang on the one nearest him and the two went down together in the yellow dust.

They rolled over and over. First one boy was on top, then the other.

"Go to it, Neddy!" shouted the taller of the two boys who were looking on.

"Muss up his pretty ruffles!" called the fat boy.

They rolled over and over. First one boy was on top,
then the other.

"Punch his face for him!" called another.

"Teach him not to come riding up here like a
prince!"

"I might have known that this would happen," said
a new voice.

It was Mr. Knox who spoke. He had been on the
terrace of his house when Alec and Christy came in
the driveway and had seen the start of the fight.

Mr. Knox jerked the two fighters apart. "Hamilton,

when will you learn to keep that temper of yours?"

"It wasn't his fault, sir, really it wasn't," said the boy they called Neddy. "We jumped on him."

"I got mad, too," said Alec.

The two boys looked at each other over their fast-swelling bruises.

"Sorry," said Neddy Stevens.

"Sorry," said Alec.

"I'll help you get your horse," said Neddy.

"Oh, he'll come when I whistle," said Alec.

"He will! Let's see him do it," one of the other boys demanded. Alec gave two quick, shrill whistles. Christy whinnied and came trotting back to where Alec was standing.

"Gee, he's grand!" said Neddy Stevens. "May I ride him?"

"Of course," answered Alec. "Do you want to now?"

Neddy shook his head but took hold of the reins. Christy laid back his ears and snapped with his big teeth. Neddy jumped back. Inside Alec was pleased, but he said nothing and they all walked along the road together.

Mr. Knox took them to the back stoop, where they washed in an iron basin. When they finished, they all went into the schoolroom in the minister's study.

Each boy had a space in the bookcase to keep his

belongings. There were no desks. Neddy Stevens, the boy who had fought with Alec, sat on a broken-down sofa with Ben Yard, the taller boy. Tom Stevens, the oldest pupil in the class, sat on a chair by the book-case. This only left a box for Alec, near the window and Mr. Knox's desk.

A pile of books was stacked on the floor. The walls of the room were of rough boards. The wind from the ocean blew the ragged curtains across Alec's face.

Mr. Knox rapped for silence.

"We'll spell first. On your feet, Neddy. See how long you can stay there."

Neddy cleared his throat.

"Themistocles," said Mr. Knox.

"T-h-e-m-i-s-t-o-c-l-e-s," he answered.

"Right," said the teacher. "Now, Caesar."

"S-e . . . . No, wait," Neddy began. "C-e-, C-a . . . ." Neddy sat down.

"How awful," said Alec to himself.

"How about you, Hamilton?" asked Mr. Knox. The boys giggled. Alec's face flushed.

"I . . . I . . . ."

"Try," urged Mr. Knox.

"I can't spell it now," answered Alec. "But I'll spell it tomorrow and any other word you want to give me in a book."

"Good," the teacher said with a frown for the rest

of the class who were tittering and whispering. "I'll expect you to keep that promise."

After spelling came Latin, history, reading, mathematics, and writing. They were all very hard for Alec. But even though the lessons were hard, Alec liked school. When it was time to go home, he wished he could stay longer.

Neddy Stevens walked with Alec to where Christy was tied.

"I'll meet you by the bridge tomorrow," Neddy called as Christy galloped off.

When he reached home, Uncle Peter was in the stable. Christy was breathing hard from his long ride.

His sides were covered with lather.

"Is that the way to treat a good horse?" said Uncle Peter sternly. "Why are you in such a hurry?"

"I want to start my studies. I'm so far behind all the others," Alec answered. "But I won't be for long."

"That is no excuse for abusing a horse. Don't let it happen again, Alec."

"I won't, sir. I really won't. I wouldn't hurt Christy for anything."

He rubbed the little horse's wet sides and covered him with a blanket. He bedded him down and waited patiently until Christy was rested enough to eat. Then he ran off to find his mother.

"Mother!" he said as he pushed open her door. "School is grand! I like Neddy Stevens best because he is a good fighter. See, here is a book Mr. Knox loaned to me. I have to learn to spell all the hard words in this chapter for tomorrow. Will you help me?" It poured out all in one breath.

After supper they began. It was very late when Alec went to bed. He went to sleep dreaming about Neddy and Mr. Knox and the school.

Chapter 9

A Great Change
for Alec

After this, Alec spent the mornings riding the cane and the afternoons in school.

At first it was very hard for him to get along with the other boys. He was used to having his own way. and he did not want to give in to anyone else.

After the lessons were over, the four boys often played soldiers up and down the drive.

"Halt!" commanded Alec one hot day.

The boys walked on until they came to some shade.

"I said, 'Halt'!" shouted Alec. "I'm captain. Why don't you obey?"

"You're always captain," said Tom crossly. "I'm not going to drill another time unless we take turns."

"But why should we take turns? I'm the best captain," argued Alec.

"You are not," said Ben Yard. "You just think you are."

"Want to prove you are better?" said Alec slipping off his coat.

"No, I don't. You always want to fight, too," said Ben. "You always like to show off. I'm tired of your fighting and bossing."

The two older boys headed back to the house. Ned stayed with Alec.

"Why do you always want to boss, Alec?" Ned asked.

"Because I'm better than the rest of you," said Alec.

"Alec," Neddy answered, "why don't you let the other fellows say that? It would sound better."

"I don't care how it sounds. I'm better and I know it."

The two boys started up toward the house. They saw Mr. Knox showing something shiny to the other boys. It glittered in the sunlight.

Alec and Neddy ran toward the others.

"This is a sword which was used by one of my ancestors in the battle of the Spanish Armada in 1588," Mr. Knox said to his students.

The boys handled it carefully. It was short and broad and very dull. But when Alec took it in his hands he felt as if he were a real officer in the King's Navy.

"I'm captain today," said Alec. "May I use it?"

"You're not," said Tom. "It is my turn and you know it."

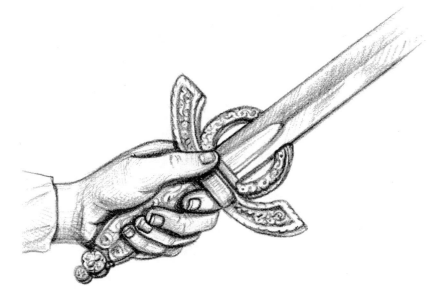

"This is a sword which was used by one of my ancestors
in the battle of the Spanish Armada in 1588,"
Mr. Knox said to his students.

"But I'm much—"

"Boys," said Mr. Knox firmly, "whoever uses this
sword will have to earn the honor. I'll choose the one
who may carry it for the day."

"What will we have to do to be captain?" asked
Alec.

"You will have to learn the first principles of being
a good officer. You will have to be willing to take
orders as well as to give them."

Alec closed his mouth firmly. He made up his mind
that he would carry the sword every day.

But it was Neddy, more often than anyone else, who had the honor. Alec's hot temper was still his worst enemy.

◆

Alec was eleven years old, but he was still very small and thin. He knew an old sailor who lived near the dock. This red-faced man taught him how to fight and Mr. Knox taught him how to fence. He worked as hard in trying to become strong as he did in everything else. Even though he was smaller than the others, he could hold his own.

Alec also worked very hard in school. He read more books than any of the other boys. He read them out loud to his mother. They discussed the stories and characters. They kept lists of words that came in the lessons and took turns in looking up their meaning.

"Alec," his mother said to him one evening when they were out on the balcony looking at the big stars overhead. "I want you to remember something very important about school."

"What is it, Mother?"

"I want you to remember that school teaches you how to think and where to look for the answers to your problems. It tells you what *others* have discovered, but it leaves *you* to explore many, many things for yourself."

"I know that, Mother. I won't stop with what other people have done. I know that you want me to go ahead and do great things for myself. I know that you want me to go away to college. I know that you want me to be either a great statesman or a historian. I'm going to do all those things. I really am."

Alec meant what he said. He asked questions of everyone he met. He watched how different people conducted their business and he learned all about the storms and the sea and the fishing trade.

Later that year, his mother became very ill and soon died. Uncle Peter was going on a trip and would be away for a year, so Alec went to live with his Uncle and Aunt Mitchell in Christiansted. Poleon, old Poleon, Hurry-Up, and Christy went with him, but life was very different for Alec.

Chapter 10

Alec's New Home

The Mitchells, Alec's aunt and uncle, lived in a large house on the main street of Christiansted.

When Alec arrived, he was given a big room facing the ocean. Just outside the window there was a balcony much like the one at home. Alec was glad of this because he had always liked to go out on the one at Uncle Peter's to watch what was going on outside.

The first evening after he came to his new home, he stepped out of his window on the little porch to watch the sun go down.

He saw the soldiers on parade at the red fort on the hill. He heard the bugler play. He saw the English flag lowered and the men march inside the enclosure.

The field slaves began to come in from the plantations. They looked tired and sang to keep their spirits up. Alec knew their songs. The music made him more homesick than anything else.

Dinner also made him long for his old home. He

had to wear a dark suit, a blouse with white ruffles, and a broad tie for his hair, and new shoes with silver buckles.

The next day Alec went back to school. He tried hard to study but he could not keep his mind on his work. He missed his mother and his early-morning rides. He wanted to go back to the old plantation.

Mr. Knox understood. He urged Alec to take Christy and go for long rides. Alec took his books with him.

One day, when he was coming home by a narrow road which was far out of town, he came upon an old two-wheeled ox cart, broken down. It was so heavy that the tired oxen could not move it from the center of the road.

The driver of the cart was beating the poor animals with long crackling whips. Alec couldn't stand by and see such cruelty.

He sprang off Christy's back and walked up to the broken wagon. He saw deep, narrow ditches on both sides of the road. The waiting traffic could not go around the cart through the field.

Several drivers from other wagons joined the first and began to beat the already worn-out oxen.

"Stop that!" shouted Alec. "What good does that do? You know that those animals can't drag that weight. We'll have to think of something else."

. . .he came upon an old two-wheeled ox cart,
broken down.

The men were so astonished at Alec's tone that they stopped whipping the oxen and watched Alec. He was still small and thin. In his suit and big hat, he looked even younger than he was. The men began to laugh.

Alec thought fast. His eyes came upon the great wooden wheels of the cart. They were solid wood and very thick. They were seven feet in diameter. The ditches were narrow.

"We'll make bridges with the wheels," shouted Alec.

The men looked at one another and went on laughing.

Alec's eyes snapped. He bit his lip and dug his nails into the palms of his hands. He knew that he must not lose his temper if he wanted these men to listen.

"I'll help you," he shouted. "If you will do as I say I'll soon have you on your way. But it will take a lot of you to help."

Even though everyone thought Alec just a child, he had already begun to have a power over the people with whom he talked. The men looked at one another, but they came to lift the great heavy wheels.

Alec guided them. He told some of the drivers to dig enough dirt to fill under the wheels when they were put across the ditch. He showed them how to bank the dirt so that the wheels would not slip.

When the work was done, Alec mounted Christy and was the first to cross the new bridge. The little horse didn't like the unsteadiness of the boards. But he trusted Alec. And Alec guided him across and around the fields.

A shout went up from the crowds as Alec came back again to the road. One carriage followed the other. One by one they all crossed the bridge and went on their way.

Alec was still standing, talking to some of the drivers when a short, heavy-set man with a black cigar in his mouth came up to where he stood.

"That was good head work, my boy," he said. "What is your name?"

"I am Alexander Hamilton, Mr. Cruger," answered Alec.

"You know who I am?" said the older man in surprise.

"Everyone knows you, sir. After all, you are the owner of the biggest warehouse on the island," said Alec.

"When you are older," the merchant said with a chuckle, "come see me about a job. I like boys who think for themselves."

Chapter 11

I Must Make Some Money

Alec watched the merchant drive away. Then he turned Christy from the road to the shore path.

On a nice day like this, he knew he would find the boys and Mr. Knox having lessons on the sand

It was a steep path to the sand. Alec saw Tom and Ben sitting on some rocks listening to Neddy, who was almost shouting.

"I never want to leave the West Indies. I have all the school I want right here. But Father says I have to go to college and—"

"To college!" shouted Alec as he hurried up to the group. "To college? Where? When?"

"Tomorrow," said Neddy, walking to meet his friend. "The family have known about it for a long time but they didn't tell me until today."

"But where are you going?" asked Alec.

"To New York in the American Colonies."

"You don't want to go?" said Alec, amazed.

"Of course I don't. I have all the school that I want right here," Neddy answered.

"Come, boys," called Mr. Knox. "We must go on with the lessons so that tomorrow we can go down to the boat to see Neddy off."

The group settled down. They began to study.

Suddenly Alec threw his book across the sand.

"I'm going to ask the captain of your boat if I can work my way across the ocean on his boat!" he shouted as he jumped up and ran to where Christy was tied.

Mr. Knox called to him. But he galloped off across the sand and up the path to the town road.

When he reached the dock, the captain of the sailing vessel was busy directing the loading of the boat. Alec stood for a minute and watched him. He was checking a list.

"I could do that for you," Alec said suddenly.

The ruddy-faced man turned around to see who had spoken.

"And why would you do my work for me, m'lad?" he asked.

"I'll do that work and as much more as you want me to do, if you will just let me go with you to the American Colonies."

The captain smiled. Boys often came to him, wanting to sail. But most of them didn't look and speak as Alec did.

"And why are ye so bent on goin' aboard?" he asked.

"I want to go to college in New York. I don't have the money to pay my passage. I want to work for it. May I?"

The captain shook his head.

"You're much too young to be goin' off by yourself to college," he said gruffly. "I could not take you."

Alec started to argue. But the big man turned away and began giving orders. Alec knew that he would not change his mind.

He went back to school. The next day he stood with the others on the dock and watched Neddy sail off to New York.

But when the others called to him and said they were going on a picnic, he shook his head.

"I can't," he called. "I have something else I have to do."

But he didn't really have something else to do. He didn't want the boys to see how upset he felt about Neddy going. He also wanted to think up a plan to make some money—lots of money. Now that Neddy was there he wanted more than ever to go to New York.

Mr. Cruger's carts began to pass. He pulled Christy over to the side of the road to let them go by.

He remembered the first time that he had noticed

those wagons and the young man who was checking the goods that came off the *Queen Bess.*

"I wonder how much he gets for doing that job," Alec said as he rode along. "I don't suppose he gets very much but—"

He jerked Christy to a stop. The little horse reared.

"I could do it. I know I could," Alec said to himself as he quieted Christy. "I'd hate it. I know I would hate being inside that dark smelly old warehouse, but if I could make money I wouldn't mind."

He patted Christy and started on a gallop down the road.

"Mr. Cruger said for me to come and see him about a job. I know he meant when I'm older but I could do that job. I can 'figger.'"

Several people called to Alec as he raced through the streets of the town, but he went by without seeing them.

He hitched Christy outside the low one-storied building, brushed off his coat, and smoothed his hair. He took a big breath of the outdoor air, then hurried into the dark office and warehouse of the Cruger Company.

For a minute he could see nothing. His eyes were used to sunlight, and it was dark and close inside. Here and there about the big room, lamps were burning. He wondered where he would find Mr. Cruger. Then he saw him in the light of the center lamp.

He sat at a high desk, shouting orders to those who hurried about him.

Alec waited. No one spoke to him. The carts began to come in. Men moved away to help unload. For a few minutes Mr. Cruger was by himself. Alec took a long breath and hurried to his side.

Alec stood by the desk, but Mr. Cruger did not look up.

"Good afternoon, sir," Alec said.

"Hummmmm," answered Mr. Cruger.

Alec waited and watched as he added up column after column of figures. He stood first on one foot and then on another.

"Mr. Cruger—"

The owner of the warehouse only frowned.

Alec stood as quietly as he could. Several men came up to talk to Mr. Cruger, but still the great man didn't say a word to Alec.

Alec was used to having people pay attention to him. He cleared his throat. Then his temper began to rise. He thought it very rude for the older man not at least to speak to him.

"I'll not stay another minute," he said to himself. "I'll go somewhere else."

Then Alec thought of the trip he wanted to take.

"I'm the one who wants the job," he thought. "Here I am losing my temper again. That would be the worst thing I could do. I'll wait him out. And I won't get mad." Alec swallowed hard. He unclenched his fists and began to grin.

"I won't lose my temper. He can't make me."

Now that he had made up his mind, he looked around him. He watched the men coming and going. He wondered what was in all the bundles on the carts.

"So," said Mr. Cruger. "You don't mind waiting? Is that it?"

"Oh, yes, I do," said Alec in surprise. "But I came to get a job and I can wait if I have to."

Mr. Cruger laughed.

"You want a job here? How old are you?"

"I'm thirteen. But I can do your work. I want a hard job which will pay me well. I want to go to college in New York."

"I see. I see," said Mr. Cruger. "What's your name? I seem to have seen you . . . . Oh, yes, you were the boy who straightened out the trouble on the back road, weren't you?"

"Yes, sir. You told me to come to you for a job."

"I said when you are grown. We have no boy's jobs."

"Then I will do a man's. I can. May I add those

figures for you?"

"So you can 'figger,' can you?" Mr. Cruger said as he got slowly down from his stool. "Those are hard sums. See you don't make a mistake if you want a job."

"I won't," Alec said quickly. "I'm good at figures."

Mr. Cruger watched the way Alec added. He didn't use his fingers as he, Mr. Cruger, had to. The merchant smiled and nodded as he saw the results of Alec's work.

"So you think you are good at figures, do you?"

"I know I am, sir. I'm good at whatever I try."

Mr. Cruger puffed on his cigar.

"Did anyone ever tell you that was no way to talk about yourself?" he asked.

"Yes, sir. Many times. But it's true and I have no one else here to speak for me. I must have the job."

Mr. Cruger nodded.

"You'll do. I like a man who is sure of himself."

Alec was happy. Mr. Cruger had called him a man. And he was going to get the job.

The merchant called for Mr. Andrews. The tall young clerk did not remember Alec.

"Take Mr. Hamilton to your department. Put him on the receiving desk."

"But Mr. Cruger—"

"You heard me," said the short man with a frown.

Mr. Cruger watched the way Alec added.

Mr. Andrews started off. But Alec didn't follow.

"Don't you want the job after all?" Mr. Cruger said.

"Yes, sir. But I would like to know how much I will be paid for my work."

"You would? Now look here, my boy, I'll attend to that when I see your work. I'm a fair man. You'll have to make do with that or get out!" he shouted.

"Yes, sir," Alec answered.

He knew he could get no further. Mr. Andrews was gone, but Alec hurried after him.

"I'll be so good that he will have to pay me a lot of money," Alec said to himself as he saw Mr. Andrews.

"What's that?" the clerk asked.

"Nothing. What shall I do first?" Alec asked.

"Sit down there and keep quiet," Mr. Andrews said with a frown. "I don't have time to teach children."

Alec sat down.

Chapter 12

Trouble Ahead

Alec's day at the warehouse began at five in the morning. At first he tried to keep up with his lessons in the evening, but he found that he was too tired to do both jobs well. He gave up school, but not his reading.

He took a book with him. When he had a few minutes, he would settle down and read until the next job appeared.

This caused problems for Alec. He was always finished first and made no mistakes. When he was finished with his work, he would not sit with the others, chatting and talking on the dock. The clerks resented Alec more and more as the days went on.

One morning he finished earlier than usual. A large closet stood at the end of the room. No one kept it in order. The day before Mr. Cruger had asked that something be found on one of the shelves. It was not to be found.

"Get that closet cleaned out!" the merchant had shouted.

But he said it to no one in particular. Now Alec found time on his hands and went to work.

Caxton, the clerk next to him, knocked over a pile of articles which Alec had put neatly outside the closet. Alec heard him laughing with the other men about how he had done it.

"The little snip," he said. "I showed him up. Thinks he's so smart."

Mr. Cruger came by to find the merchandise scattered all over the floor.

"Who put these here?" he shouted.

"Hamilton, sir," said Caxton.

Alec's face burned. He clenched his hands.

"Pick them up, Hamilton. Don't let that happen again."

Alec hurried with the extra job and went back to the closet he had just cleaned. It was a big mess again.

Caxton was just coming out of the closet with some nails in his hands.

Several days later Alec's file sheets were incorrectly added. Mr. Cruger looked at him in surprise when he called Alec in about the mistake.

"You had better be more careful, Hamilton. I thought that you didn't make mistakes."

Alec couldn't understand. He was sure that he had checked his figures.

In this warehouse, the clerks left the day's reports on their desks for the head clerk to collect. Alec was usually finished early and went off to do something else.

A week later the same thing happened. This time the mistake was so large that the difference meant many dollars.

"Hamilton," Mr. Cruger said as he handed Alec the incorrect sheet. "How did this happen?"

Alec's face was serious. He shook his head.

"I don't know, sir. Of course I can add. I wonder—"

Alec stopped.

"You wonder what, my boy?" Mr. Cruger asked.

"May I bring my sheet to you directly when I'm finished?" he asked.

"You may," answered Mr. Cruger grimly.

The first time that Alec took his finished sheet to the head desk, Caxton frowned.

"You'll keep your mouth shut, if you know what's good for you," he said to Alec.

Alec said nothing, but his lists were correct from then on.

Alec was soon made the assistant head clerk, and at the end of three months he was the head clerk with ten men under him.

But, Alec wasn't happy. He had always been

One evening a letter finally came from Neddy.

among people who liked him. Now, though ten men did as he told them to do, he knew that none of them were his friends. It made the work hard, and it made Alec unhappy.

One evening a letter finally came from Neddy. Alec rushed over to Mr. Knox's with it in his hand.

"A letter from Neddy!" he shouted.

It was after hours and Mr. Knox was sitting on his terrace reading.

"When was it written?" he called.

"March 14, 1770. Two months ago. Neddy's been so busy he couldn't write. They are having a lot of trouble in New York and Boston, he says," Alec answered.

Mr. Knox read the letter.

"I wish I were over there. Neddy says that he doesn't know who is right, the King or the colonists. I'd soon find out if I were there," Alec said, pacing up and down the terrace.

"It is something to do with taxes," Alec went on. "What right has the King to tax Englishmen unless the citizens themselves decide what is the right amount?"

"That is the question which is going to start a great deal of trouble in the new country. I wish I were going to be there to see the finish. I hope that you will be," said Mr. Knox.

"I don't see how I'll get there. I'm making more money all the time, but not enough."

"Have you ever asked your uncles? They might give it to you."

"But I could never let them support me. No, I must make it. I will, too."

Alec continued to work at the warehouse. Some of the men began to like Alec for who he was. They began to see that he wished to make their work run more smoothly, too.

Then, when Alec was fourteen, Mr. Cruger put him in charge of the warehouse in Christiansted and made him overseer of all the others on the other islands. Mr. Cruger was going to go to America for a lengthy trip.

Alec's uncles went to Mr. Cruger to object.

"He is too young," they said. "He has no experience."

"I know what I'm doing, my friends," Mr. Cruger said. "You need not worry. I have confidence in Alexander. He is a most unusual boy."

The next two years were the most interesting yet in Alec's life.

His work took him on many trips about the islands of the West Indies. This was the part of the job that he enjoyed most.

He met many different kinds of people. At first when the men saw how young this representative for Cruger was, they tried to take advantage of him.

But this lasted only a short time. He made the men feel that they too were responsible for the business. They grew to like Alec.

When Mr. Cruger returned he was so pleased with the way the work had been handled that he offered Alec a full partnership, though he was only sixteen.

"I can't, Mr. Cruger," Alec said seriously. "I would like it if I were to stay here, but I'm going to go to college."

His uncles and everyone but Mr. Knox urged Alec to reconsider. Alec only shook his head.

"Something will happen sometime," he said, "that will help me to make the money to go."

Something so exciting did happen that it changed his whole life. Something that the West Indies never forgot.

Chapter 13

The Hurricane

It was late August. The weather had been hot and dry. There was a great deal of sickness on the island.

Poleon acted grumpy and distracted. Alec noticed and asked him what the matter was.

"Master Alec, I'm thinking about this hurricane hitting this island," he replied.

"What do you mean, Poleon? Have you been listening to those stable boys again?" asked Alec.

"Look at the clouds up there, Master. Listen to that booming of the ocean on the rocks. Feel that wind whistling through the palm trees."

Alec grabbed for his hat, but the wind caught it up and sent it sailing across the road. Poleon scrambled after it and came back looking more worried than ever.

Alec patted him on the shoulder and mounted Christy.

"Poleon, you don't have to worry. You know that if

there is any danger the fort guns will send us a signal," Alec said, as he rode off to the warehouse.

As he cantered along the rough street, he heard a sudden noise behind him. Men were shouting. Alec pulled over to the side of the road just as a heavy cart with two oxen clattered by. It was the first time in all his life that Alec had seen oxen going faster than a walk.

Across the street he saw a man putting up heavy wooden shutters.

"I don't like the look of the weather, Mr. Hamilton," the man said. "Remember the old saying about the hurricane?"

'June, too soon,
July, stand by,
August, come it must,
September, remember,
October, all over.'

"It's almost the end of August and the wind hasn't changed direction for twenty-four hours."

Alec rode on. He shook himself. He felt shivers run up and down his spine. A dog, barking at a cat on a fence, suddenly stopped and ran off yelping with its tail between its legs.

"Oh, it's all foolishness," said Alec to himself. "I

wish it would rain and clear the air."

But when he reached the store, even Mr. Cruger was standing outside looking at the sky. This gave Alec the strangest feeling of all. Mr. Nicholas Cruger never wasted time during office hours.

"The signs are all against us, Hamilton," he said. "The *Susan Meed* is due today or tomorrow. She carries a very valuable cargo. I only hope she lands before the storm breaks."

The two went inside together.

Alec bent his head over his ledger. The morning wore on. Noon came. The wind blew steadily from the west. Alec hurried down to the docks. Not a dock worker was there to help land the *Susan Meed* if she did come in.

The ocean looked oily. Great swells were rolling in from far out in the harbor. The wind seemed less, but it still blew. The gulls sat hunched up on the end of the dock. None were flying.

Suddenly, the sound of a cannon, booming in the distance, came through the stillness. Cold chills ran up and down Alec's back. *"Boom, boom, boom,"* came the sound. Again and again the booming came—three, four, five, six, and then seven times.

Seven was the hurricane signal from the fort. It meant that St. Croix would be in the direct route of the storm.

Someone shouted from down the street. Men and women ran in and out of their houses.

The signal they all dreaded had come.

Alec ran for the warehouse.

Inside the warehouse everyone was working to put up the shutters.

He pulled himself up, waited for a minute until the squall
of wind was over, and then hurried out to where
Christy was bucking and rearing.

"We must notify the planters," Mr. Cruger said. "You
have your horse outside, Hamilton. Take the bay road.
We have at least an hour before the storm strikes."

Now that they knew what was before them, Mr.

Cruger was calm. Alec felt better, too. He ran for the door and jerked it open. The wind struck him full in the face. He fell down as if he had been hit with a club.

He pulled himself up, waited for a minute until the squall of wind was over, and then hurried out to where Christy was bucking and rearing. Poleon held his halter, and was trying to calm him.

"What did I tell you, Master?" he said.

"What are you doing here, Poleon? Why aren't you home helping close the house?" shouted Alec over the noise of the wind.

"I'm going with you and Christy."

"Get up behind then. Quick now!" Alec shouted.

Christy reared and broke for the road. He was not used to carrying two people on his back.

It began to rain. At the corner of the street, the wind caught them. The horse snorted and reared.

The noise around them was terrible. Stones from the roofs of the small houses were flying through the air.

"We're going to have trouble!" Alec shouted, although he knew that Poleon could not hear him.

They passed other messengers on the way across the island to warn and help their neighbors.

At the edge of the town, these messengers separated.

Alec turned Christy to the outside road lined with

beautiful palm trees.

These giants were bending as if they were young saplings. There was a sudden crack and the sound of splintering wood.

"Look out!" shouted Poleon.

A great tree brushed past them and fell directly across the road. It seemed as if they were surrounded by many fences.

Christy began to whinny. He plunged and snorted.

Poleon fell and, as he fell, he pulled Alec with him. For a minute Alec thought that the horse's hoofs would hit them.

Both boys scrambled to their feet. Alec's face was bleeding and Poleon's arm hung limp.

"We got to get along," shouted Poleon.

For a minute the wind lessened. Alec was able to make Christy hear his voice. This somewhat quieted the frightened animal. Alec helped Poleon up first. Then he sat behind him as his arm could not hold on to Alec's waist.

They went by the Stevens's plantation. All the slaves were outside their cabins, readying them for the storm.

The Lytton home came next. Uncle Peter was working with the field slaves to raise the shutters. Alec pulled Christy around.

"I've got to go on," he shouted to Poleon. "But you get off and go help Uncle Peter. I'll be right back."

Poleon slid to the ground and Alec and Christy raced away. He passed the Mathewsons', the Williams' and the Knowles'. Everyone was working in the fields. No one was ready. They ran to put up the shutters when Alec told them the hurricane was coming.

Mrs. Hawkings's small cabin was last on the road. She alone was ready. Her shutters were in place. Alec pulled Christy about.

Should he go in and stay with the old lady or try to make it back home before the storm broke?

Christy made up his mind for him. He took the bit into his teeth and, head down, bolted for home.

Before them was the terror of greenish-black clouds that swirled and banked.

Alec clung to Christy's neck.

When they came to Uncle Peter's gate, Christy swerved, slipped, and fell. Alec thought that the whole ocean was pounding and booming about him. He lay on the ground and tried to scream. The sound of his voice came back to him. He tried to get up. Then, quite without effort, he felt himself rushing through the air, spinning around and around.

Then everything went dark.

The next thing that Alec heard was Uncle Peter's voice.

Alec opened his eyes. Uncle Peter was standing by his side, but they were not out in the storm. He was in his own bed. Becca and Poleon were there, too. His head ached and he couldn't remember what had happened.

"How did I get here?" he asked.

"You were caught in the middle of the hurricane, Alec," said Uncle Peter. "You are very lucky to be alive."

"I found you, Master Alec," said Poleon. "I saw you flying through the air. That storm pitched you right into the back garden. Are you feeling better?"

Alec felt his head. It was bandaged.

"The hurricane really came this time, didn't it, Uncle Peter?" he said slowly.

"The worst hurricane that has ever been recorded over the West Indies," said Uncle Peter. "We will never forget the storm of August 1773."

Chapter 14

A Dream Come True

When Alec woke the next day, he was still so sore that he could barely move. He thought that his bones must all be broken. He was black and blue from his head to his feet.

Christy was so tired that he stood with his head down, begging not to be taken out of the stable.

On the second morning after the hurricane, Alec rode into Christiansted.

All along the road, houses had been knocked about like toys. Great forest trees were lying, uprooted, across the way.

Alec found Mr. Knox in his church. The steeple had fallen through the roof. The minister was trying to clear up enough so that he could have a service.

As the two worked, Alec told the older man all that had happened to him up to the point when he fell from Christy's back.

"After that, I have to rely on Poleon's story. I can't remember a thing."

Mr. Knox listened intently. Then he handed Alec a piece of paper.

"Write it all down, just as you have told it to me," he said. "I want it before you forget a single incident."

The minister left Alec writing the story. He had other tasks. Alec left the story on Mr. Knox's desk.

Then he hurried off to the warehouse to see what had happened there.

Mr. Cruger looked tired but very glad to see his young assistant. The men were all glad to see Alec, too. It made him feel good to see that they no longer resented him.

For days they all worked together. The back end of the building was entirely gone. The docks had collapsed into the bay. The main street of the town was blocked by fallen trees. Everyone was busy.

Then one night, after two weeks of work, Mr. Cruger sent Alec home.

"Stay until you are really rested," he said.

Alec went to bed at noon, and it was the next night before he woke up. He had some supper and went back to bed again.

The next morning, he heard Poleon out in the hall talking to Aunt Mitchell.

"Master Alec sure can sleep, can't he, Miss Anna?

Won't he be surprised when Mr. Knox tells him the big secret?"

"Tells me what secret?" Alec shouted.

Poleon came to the door. He was grinning.

"I can't say that, Master Alec," he said. "But you better get yourself down to Preacher Knox's. He's got something to tell you."

Alec smiled. He didn't hurry, but after he had his breakfast, he mounted Christy and trotted off.

When he came to Mr. Knox's house, he heard Uncle Mitchell's voice. Then Uncle Peter spoke and Mr. Knox joined in. They all seemed very excited.

They mentioned Alec's name.

"I wish he would come," Uncle Peter said. "I can hardly wait until he hears the news."

"I'm here," Alec called.

The three men came to the door. They were all smiling.

"Come in, nephew," said Uncle Peter.

"What is it? I know something must have happened. Please tell me," Alec urged.

Mr. Knox took a small paper from his pocket.

"This," he said, "is your ticket to New York."

Alec grabbed the paper. It was the small newspaper which was published on St. Kitts Island. His story about the hurricane was printed on the first page.

"But I don't understand! New York—what do you

mean? Please tell me," Alec said.

Then all three of the men began to talk at once.

"The editor of this paper wanted you to come and work for him. He says you have a great future in writing," said Uncle Peter. "But . . . ."

"Mr. Knox said that you would rather . . . ."

"I said that you had always wanted to go to college in New York, so . . . ."

"Your Uncle Peter and I have decided to . . . ."

"We are going to lend you the money to make the trip and to stay in college," said Uncle Mitchell.

"Alec," Mr. Knox said proudly, "you have won your chance to go."

"So, it really was the hurricane that gave me my chance to go to the Colonies?" said Alec with a shaky laugh.

"I guess that is right," said Uncle Peter.

"But the money. I . . . ."

"We said we will loan you the money, Alec," said Uncle Peter, "if you want it to be that way. You can pay it all back. We thought there was a good future for you on the Island. But now we believe you can do bigger things and should have your chance."

Then, to everyone's surprise, Alec turned and ran back to Christy. Without looking back, he galloped off toward the Cliff picnic grounds.

It was several hours later before he returned.

"I'm sorry, Mr. Knox," he said. "I didn't know I was such a baby. I didn't want Uncle Peter and Uncle Mitchell to see me cry. You understand, don't you?"

"Of course, Alec. Now you need to make plans."

The next two days were exciting and busy. Aunt Mitchell soon had his small trunk packed. But he wanted to say goodbye to all his friends.

"I wish we could have another picnic before I go. Just Ben and Tom and you and me," said Alec.

Mr. Knox smiled.

"Wait and see," was all he would say.

That evening they had a picnic. Becca fixed all of Alec's favorite dishes for them.

The four good friends sat on the flat top of High Cliffs until very late. They talked about Alec's first day in school and the many, many good times they had had since that day. They laughed about all the fights and fusses that Neddy and Alec had had, and they talked about the future.

"You have a great future before you, Alec," said Mr. Knox. "Only remember this. It makes no difference that you came from a small island far away from the American Colonies, and that you went barefooted and had very little schooling. That should make you a more understanding man."

"Don't let that temper get loose, Alec," said Ben Yard with a smile.

"Don't pick a fight every chance you get," added Tom. "And be sure to write to us and tell us all about what you and Neddy are doing."

Alec smiled.

"I'll write whenever I can. But I expect to be awfully busy," he answered.

"Going to run the country over there?" teased Ben.

"Maybe," laughed Alec. "You never know what a West Indian will do."

Only Mr. Knox guessed that what Alec said then might come true.

After they had all parted for the night, Alec took Christy for a long ride in bright moonlight. Alec could see for miles across the little island on which he had worked and played. He could see much of the ruin which the hurricane had left.

Maybe I ought to stay and help rebuild the houses, he thought.

But he knew that he would go tomorrow, and he was sure that it was right for him to leave.

The sun was just coming up when Alec came back home.

The boat sailed at noon that day. Many of the townspeople were on the dock to see Alec go, but in all the crowd Alec could not find his three best friends. He couldn't understand their not being there to wave goodbye.

A stiff breeze carried the small boat quickly from the dock. He could no longer see the figures of those who had come to say goodbye.

The ship's bell rang. Alec hurried across the gangplank, still looking back for Mr. Knox, Ben, and Tom.

A stiff breeze carried the small boat quickly from the dock. He could no longer see the figures of those who had come to say goodbye.

From the entrance of the harbor the boat sailed close to the shore until it passed Seaforth Point. Alec leaned against the ship's rail, watching the objects he knew on shore. They were very plain now that the boat was so close to the beach. His eyes followed the winding road that led to High Cliffs.

"Hello, hello!" came shouts from land. "Alec, Alec, here we are! Goodbye!"

Then Alec began to shout, too, for there were Mr. Knox, Ben and Tom. On the minister's shoulder something fluttered. Hurry-Up was cawing too; although Alec couldn't hear his voice, he knew the parrot was calling, "Goodbye, matey!" Christy stood between Tom and Ben—they had all come to see him off.

"Goodbye, goodbye. Thank you! Goodbye!" Alec called.

Then the boat swung out into the current.

Alec watched the shore until he could no longer see his friends and then hurried up to the prow.

The salty spray blew into his face. Alec began to sing because he was so happy. He shouted with the wind that was rising. The wind caught the sound of his voice and carried it off toward the American Colonies, the land of his dreams.

What Happened Next?

• Alexander enrolled in King's College (now Columbia University) in New York City.

• Alexander Hamilton served as an aide to General Washington in 1777, during the American Revolution.

• In 1787, Alexander helped organize the Constitutional Convention that created the American Constitution.

• President Washington appointed him as the first Secretary of the Treasury in 1789. Alexander introduced plans for the first national bank (First Bank of the United States) and the United States Mint.

• In June of 1804, Aaron Burr, vice president of the United States and Hamilton's political enemy, challenged him to a duel. Alexander was killed in his duel with Burr on July 11, 1804.

For more information and further reading about
Alexander Hamilton, visit the **Young Patriots Series**
website at www.patriapress.com

Fun Facts about Alexander Hamilton

• Alexander's portrait appears on the ten-dollar bill. He is one of only two non-presidents to have his face on American currency. The other is Benjamin Franklin, who appears on the one-hundred-dollar bill.

• Alexander established one of the first two political parties in America, the Federalist Party.

• Alexander Hamilton was one of only seven foreign-born signers of the Constitution. There were 39 signers altogether.

• Alexander's face, along with 77 others, is carved into the "Million Dollar Staircase," a famous staircase located in the New York State Capitol.

• Hamilton College, named after Alexander Hamilton, is the third oldest college in New York State. Today the Alexander Hamilton Scholarship Fund helps young people from Nevis Island, the island on which Alexander was born, attend this college.

• *The New York Evening Post*, founded in 1801 by Alexander, is the oldest continually running newspaper in America.

When Alexander Hamilton Lived

Date	Event
1755–1757	Alexander was born on the British island of Nevis in the West Indies.
	• The Seven Years' War, also called the French and Indian War, began in 1756.
	• The first steam engine in the Western Hemisphere was used at a copper mine in the New Jersey colony.
1765	Alexander moved to St. Croix with his mother.
	• Britain passed the Stamp Act, which forced American colonists to pay a tax to the king for all documents, including newspapers.
	• The world's first savings bank opened in Germany.
1773	Alexander arrived in New York to attend college.
	• The colonists rebelled against the British Parliament's Tea Act through the Boston Tea Party.
	• Land surveyor George Rogers Clark, at the age of twenty-one, began laying out the city of Louisville, Kentucky.

1775	Alexander joined the American colonists' army.
	• George Washington became the leader of that army.
	• The American Revolution began with the Battles of Lexington and Concord.
1783	Alexander was elected to the Continental Congress.
	• The American Revolution ended with the Treaty of Paris.
	• The Montgolfier brothers invented the first hot-air balloon, on which the first passengers were a sheep, a rooster, and a duck.
1787	Alexander attended the Constitutional Convention.
	• Three states, Delaware, Pennsylvania, and New Jersey, ratified the Constitution.
	• Oliver Evans's automatic flour mill, invented in 1780, made white bread widely available in America.
1789	Alexander became America's first Secretary of the Treasury.
	• George Washington was elected as the first President of the United States.

- North Carolina became the twelfth state in the Union when it ratified the Constitution only after James Madison wrote the Bill of Rights (added to the Constitution in 1791).

1801   Alexander founded the *New York Evening Post.*

- The House elected Thomas Jefferson over Aaron Burr as the third President of the United States.
- John Chapman, also known as "Johnny Appleseed," began planting apple trees in the Ohio Valley.

1804   Alexander fought in a duel with Aaron Burr and was killed.

- Lewis and Clark began their expedition across the American Northwest.
- There were seventeen states in the Union.

What Does That Mean?

brandishing (p. 59)—waving or shaking

bugler (p. 70)—a person who sounds a trumpet-like instrument, usually for military calls

cantered (p. 92)—moved or rode at an easy gallop

close (p. 78)—stuffy; not open; shut in

foremen (p. 52)—the people in charge of a group of workers

gait (p. 49)—the way in which a horse moves, such as a trot, a walk, or a gallop

halter (p. 44)—a rope or strap used to lead horses

ledger (p. 93)—an account book in which one records sales and purchases

liniment (p. 48)—a liquid medication rubbed on the skin to relieve pain

prow (p. 107)—the front part of a ship

rear (p. 54)—to rise up on the hind legs

Themistocles (p. 62)—a Greek general and politician who lived in Athens during the time of the Persian Wars

About the Author

Helen Boyd Higgins was born in Columbus, Indiana in 1892. She was the author of numerous children's books, including *Juliette Low, Girl Scout Founder* in the **Young Patriots Series**, *Stephen Foster, Boy Minstrel, Noah Webster, Boy of Words, Walter Reed, Boy Who Wanted to Know,* and *Old Trails and New.* Mrs. Higgins also penned *Our Burt Lake Story.*

She was dedicated to enlightening the lives of children by presenting them with histories of significant men and women of our country.

Submitted by William Higgins

Books in the Young Patriots Series

Watch for more **Young Patriots** Coming Soon
Visit www.patriapress.com for updates!

For more information about
Alexander Hamilton, Young Statesman
and all the Young Patriots Series titles,
visit our website at:
www.patriapress.com

CPSIA information can be obtained
at www.ICGtesting.com
Printed in the USA
FSOW01n2314080217
30547FS